It was a bright and sunny autumn morning and Mam-gu Iet-wen and Bwgi-bo were clearing the flower border. Now the wheelbarrow was almost full.

Let's take this last load over to Rhoswen.

KV-191-415

The twins, Owen and Olwen, were also keen to do some work. They hoped to help Rhoswen with her Compot – her very special compost bin.

Can I help you, Rhoswen?

And me!

The Compot

There's plenty of work here for everyone.

Just then, Mam-gu Iet-wen arrived with Bwgi-bo, the silent scarecrow, and his wheelbarrow full of faded flowers.

Mam-gu Iet-wen began to help Bwgi-bo unload the wheelbarrow. She handed baskets to Owen and Olwen.

'I've brought you a wonderful pile of dead sunflowers again, Rhoswen,' said Mam-gu Iet-wen. 'Do you need a few other ingredients to make your special compost?'

I need scraps of wool...

Owen had an idea. He grabbed his basket and off he went to the fields.

There, Glanwen, the sheep, was busy sorting the wool. When she heard about the Compot she was happy to help.

Is there enough wool here for Rhoswen?

Yes. Thank you, Glanwen.

5

Back in the garden, Olwen was ready to help Rhoswen too.

I need eggshells to make my special compost.

Aha! I know where to go!

The Compot

And off Olwen raced to the hen house.

Lilwen and Dilwen, the hens, were happily clucking outside the hen house.

'Bore da, Lilwen and Dilwen. Have you any eggshells to use in the Compot, please?'

'Well, I'm not really sure about that. We also need eggshells for keeping slugs away, you know,' said Dilwen. But Lilwen wasn't happy with Dilwen's answer.

Tut, tut. Where would you be without good compost to grow your leeks, Dilwen?

Lilwen clucked kindly at Olwen and said, 'Leave your basket there for a minute. We really must help with the Compot.'

Sulwen, the slug, had heard them talking. She glowered at Dilwen. 'Huh! Keeping slugs away, indeed!' she thought.

My friends and I could do great work munching away in that Compot!

And off she slid to Mam-gu Iet-wen's garden.

Lilwen filled Olwen's basket with eggshells.

Thanks for all these shells, Lilwen. Oh, and thanks to Dilwen too.

We've kept some of the shells to put on the soil, don't worry!

Lilwen gave Olwen a secret wink.

10

Back in the garden, Bwgi-bo was dancing and clinking with excitement. What task would he be given? he wondered.

I need straw for the Compot...

Hmm?

Bwgi-bo scratched his head for a little while. Then, he remembered that Blodwen, the cow, would have straw in the cowshed!

'You'll need something bigger than a basket to carry straw, Bwgi-bo,' said Mam-gu Iet-wen. So, the scarecrow fetched the wheelbarrow.

Perfect.

i mewn

And off he went on his exciting straw-hunt.

Just outside Blodwen's dairy was a very smelly, steaming pile of straw. Bwgi-bo loaded the straw (and everything in it) into the wheelbarrow quickly and carefully.

Ych a fi! How smelly!

Hang on! Don't take it all!

Blodwen, the cow, wanted to keep some of it to protect the rhubarb plants over the winter.

Bwgi-bo pushed the heavy wheelbarrow back to the garden. The old wheel creaked and screeched – what a noise!

It sounds like a squealing pig.

squeak screech squeak

Roaster Toaster

'Oh dear. Let me take a closer look,' said Mam-gu Iet-wen.

Mam-gu Iet-wen bent down to examine the wheel through Goleuwen, her magical magnifying glass. 'Well, look who's here!' she cried.

There she saw Sulwen, the slug, and her friends. They had come to the garden to help Rhoswen.

We have important work to do now as well.

Yes indeed! We must eat!

'That's very good of you,' said Mam-gu Iet-wen. Carefully, she placed Sulwen and all her little friends inside the Compot.

As Rhoswen lifted the lid of the Compot, a beady eye was watching her. Branwen, the white crow, was spying! She wanted to learn how Rhoswen made such wonderful compost.

What have we here? A pot of cawl? Ho! Ho!

My magical mix, Branwen fach.

'If you really want to help, Branwen, fetch some twigs from Allt-wen wood,' said Mam-gu Iet-wen sternly. And off Branwen went, with no arguments.

Suddenly, Bwgi-bo started sniffing.

Are you going to sneeze, Bwgi-bo?

No. There was a wonderful smell coming from somewhere — somewhere in the garden.

Until now, nobody had noticed that Rhoswen had a little oven in the garden - her very own Roaster-Toaster! And there was something special roasting today.

What's in that Roaster-Toaster that smells so wonderful?

Roaster Toaster

Owen and Olwen followed Bwgi-bo over to the Roaster-Toaster. Bwgi-bo looked hopefully at the little oven. Was it lunchtime?

I'm so hungry, Rhoswen.

So am I.

Roaster Toaster

Rhoswen opened the oven door and showed them a plateful of plump little seeds.

Take care, the plate is very hot.

Olwen stared at the plate and tried to guess the name of the plump seeds.

What are they?

Sunflower seeds. Toasted and roasted. Nothing better.

Olwen was so glad that Mam-gu Iet-wen had gathered the dead sunflower heads. As for Rhoswen, what a clever little pig she was to have roasted the seeds in her Roaster-Toaster!

Everyone began to nibble at the tasty seeds.

They're like nuts.

Except they're warm. Yummy!

'Thank you, Rhoswen,' said Mam-gu Iet-wen. Bwgi-bo wiggled and clinked to show how much he enjoyed them too. Everyone just loved the sunflower seeds.

Suddenly, there came a screech from above.

Branwen! What's happening?

Don't forget me!

The white crow's beak was full of twigs for the Compot. And yes, there were tasty sunflower seeds for her as well.

There were more seeds in the Roaster-Toaster, ready to give to friends who had helped.

A little gift for EVERYONE who helped.

The Compot was full now, and so were the tummies. Rhoswen was very happy.

Everyone had worked very hard with the recycling. All of Iet-wen's garden waste was in the Compot and none of it had gone in the rubbish lorry.

Yes indeed!

Roasting and composting is such fun!

There's plenty of compost here for the whole garden! thought Bwgi-bo.

He could hardly wait for next year, when bright new sunflowers would grow in Mam-gu Iet-wen's garden once again.

'We've all done our very best to keep the world clean and green!' explained Mam-gu Iet-wen and she gave all her friends a big cwtsh.

Thanks, my friends!

Yes, ALL our friends. Diolch yn fawr!

First published in 2015 by Gomer Press, Llandysul, Ceredigion, SA44 4JL
www.gomer.co.uk

ISBN 978 1 84851 861 2
ISBN 978 1 84851 929 9 (ePUB)
ISBN 978 1 84851 941 1 (Kindle)

Copyright text and illustrations: Llinos Mair © 2015

All rights reserved. No part of this book may be reproduced, stored in a retrieval system,
or transmitted in any form or by any means, electronic, electrostatic, magnetic tape, mechanical, photocopying,
recording or otherwise, without the permission in writing from the publishers.

Part funded by the Welsh Government as part of its Welsh and bilingual teaching and learning resources
commissioning programme.

Ariennir yn Rhannol gan
Lywodraeth Cymru
Part Funded by
Welsh Government

Printed and bound in Wales by Gomer Press, Llandysul, Ceredigion, SA44 4JL

AB   9 FEB 20

AB

Rhif/No. _____ Dosb./Class _____ JF

Dylid dychwelyd neu adnewyddu'r eitem erbyn neu cyn y dyddiad a nodir uchod.
Oni wneir hyn gellir codi tal.

This book is to be returned or renewed on or before the last date stamped above,
otherwise a charge may be made.

Wenfro
O! Gwyn ein byd
- a gwyrdd!

GW 6273326 5

Llyfrgelloedd Mon, Conwy & Gwynedd Libraries	
Askews & Holts	
AB	9 FEB 2016